My Color Praises

Crystal Bowman

Illustrated by
Claudine Gévry

BakerBooks
Grand Rapids, Michigan

red

The RED rose in my garden

Has just begun to grow.

I praise God for his beauty

As seasons come and go.

Flowers are appearing on the earth.
The season for singing has come. Song of Songs 2:12

green

Lord, you make the bright GREEN grass

From just a tiny seed.

I praise you that you make all things

And know just what they need.

If that is how God dresses the wild grass,
won't he dress you even better? Matthew 6:30

gold

Just like honey, GOLD and sweet,

God's words are sweet and true.

I praise God for the Bible—

His words for me and you.

They are sweeter than honey that is taken from the honeycomb.
Psalm 19:10

gray

GRAY clouds in the afternoon
Bring water to the ground.
I praise God for his love for me
As raindrops sprinkle down.

Your faithfulness reaches to the clouds.
Psalm 57:10 NLT

orange

ORANGE juice in the morning—
Mom makes it just for me.
I praise you, God, for mothers,
And for my family.

LORD, *in the morning you hear my voice.*
In the morning I pray to you. Psalm 5:3

brown

The rich BROWN earth belongs to God,

For he alone is King.

He rules from heaven with his love,

And so I shout and sing.

God is the King of the whole earth.
Sing a psalm of praise to him. Psalm 47:7

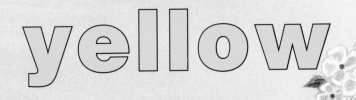

yellow

The YELLOW sun is rising;

It glows in the morning sky.

Oh, God, you are so awesome!

I lift your name on high.

*He calls out to the earth from the sunrise in the east
to the sunset in the west. Psalm 50:1*

blue

I look into the big BLUE sky
To see creation's story.
I praise God for the heavens
That tell about his glory.

The heavens tell about the glory of God.
The skies show that his hands created them.
Psalm 19:1

black

Every night it's BLACK outside,

And then it's time for bed.

I sing a happy bedtime song;

I pray and bow my head.

During the night I sing about him.
I say a prayer to the God who gives me life. Psalm 42:8

purple

God made the PURPLE mountains

So big and strong and tall.

Oh, Lord, you are so powerful—

You're greater than us all!

You formed the mountains by your power.
You showed how strong you are. Psalm 65:6

See all the pretty colors?
God made the world so bright.
Give thanks for his creation,
And praise him day and night.

Crystal Bowman is a lyricist, poet, and author of thirty books for children, including the Little Blessing Series for children. She's also written a women's devotional, *Meditations for Moms*. As a former preschool director and teacher with a background in early childhood development and education, she still makes many school presentations and loves reading to children. Her two books of humorous poetry, *Cracks in the Sidewalk* and *If Peas Could Taste Like Candy* are favorites in the classroom. Crystal is involved in MOPS (Mothers of Preschoolers) as a writer and speaker. She and her husband live in Michigan and are the parents of three grown children.

Claudine Gévry is a children's book illustrator who lives with her Japanese nightingale named Fuji in Montreal, Canada. Her work is published by Candlewick Press, Harcourt, Scholastic, Time Life Books, Publications International, and *Weekly Reader,* as well as Monotype Composition, MSC International, and Canada's Ciel d'images and Tye Sil Corp. A visual arts graduate from the University of Quebec, and the daughter of a writer, Claudine has always loved books, though she began her career in television—illustrating and art directing an animated film for the National Film Board of Canada.

Text © 2004 by Crystal Bowman
Illustrations © 2004 by Claudine Gévry

Published by Baker Books
a division of Baker Publishing Group
P.O. Box 6287, Grand Rapids, MI 49516-6287
www.bakerbooks.com

Printed in the United States of America

Published in association with the literary agency of Ann Spangler and Company, 1420
Pontiac Road Southeast, Grand Rapids, Michigan 49506.

Library of Congress Cataloging-in-Publication Data is on file at the Library of
Congress, Washington, D.C.

ISBN 0-8010-4514-2

Unless otherwise indicated, Scripture is taken from the HOLY BIBLE, NEW
INTERNATIONAL READER'S VERSION™. Copyright © 1995, 1996, 1998 by
International Bible Society. Used by permission of Zondervan. All rights reserved.

Scripture marked NLT is taken from the *Holy Bible,* New Living Translation, copyright
© 1996. Used by permission of Tyndale House Publishers, Inc., Wheaton, Illinois
60189. All rights reserved.

The illustrations in this book were rendered in soft pastel.
The text type is set in Utopia.
The display type is set in Helvetica.

Art Direction by Paula Gibson
Design by Brian Brunsting

Colors, colors everywhere!

How many do you know?

Point to them and say each one—

Get ready, get set, go!

purple

See the lovely PURPLE cloth
So bright and smooth and pretty?
Lydia sold it to her friends
While walking through the city.

Acts 16:13–15

black

The sky was BLACK from noon till three
The day that Jesus died.
"He surely was the Son of God!"
A Roman soldier cried.

Mark 15:33–39

blue

Bouncy, choppy big BLUE waves

Were splashing in the sea

Where Jesus met some fishermen

And said, "Come follow me!"

Mark 1:16–20

yellow

The YELLOW straw was soft and warm
That filled the manger bed
Where baby Jesus lay asleep
Just like the angel said.

Luke 2:7–16

brown

Nehemiah loved the Lord;

He fixed the big BROWN wall.

And then the holy Word of God

Was read to one and all.

Nehemiah 6:15–16; 8:1–8

orange

ORANGE fire came down from heaven
And burned the stones and boards.
Elijah wanted all to know
Our God is Lord of Lords.

1 Kings 18:17–39

gray

David took a smooth GRAY stone
And slung it round and round.
It hit Goliath in the head—
The giant came tumbling down.

1 Samuel 17

gold

The people made a calf of GOLD
While Moses was away.
It made God very angry
When the people sinned that day.

Exodus 32:1–10

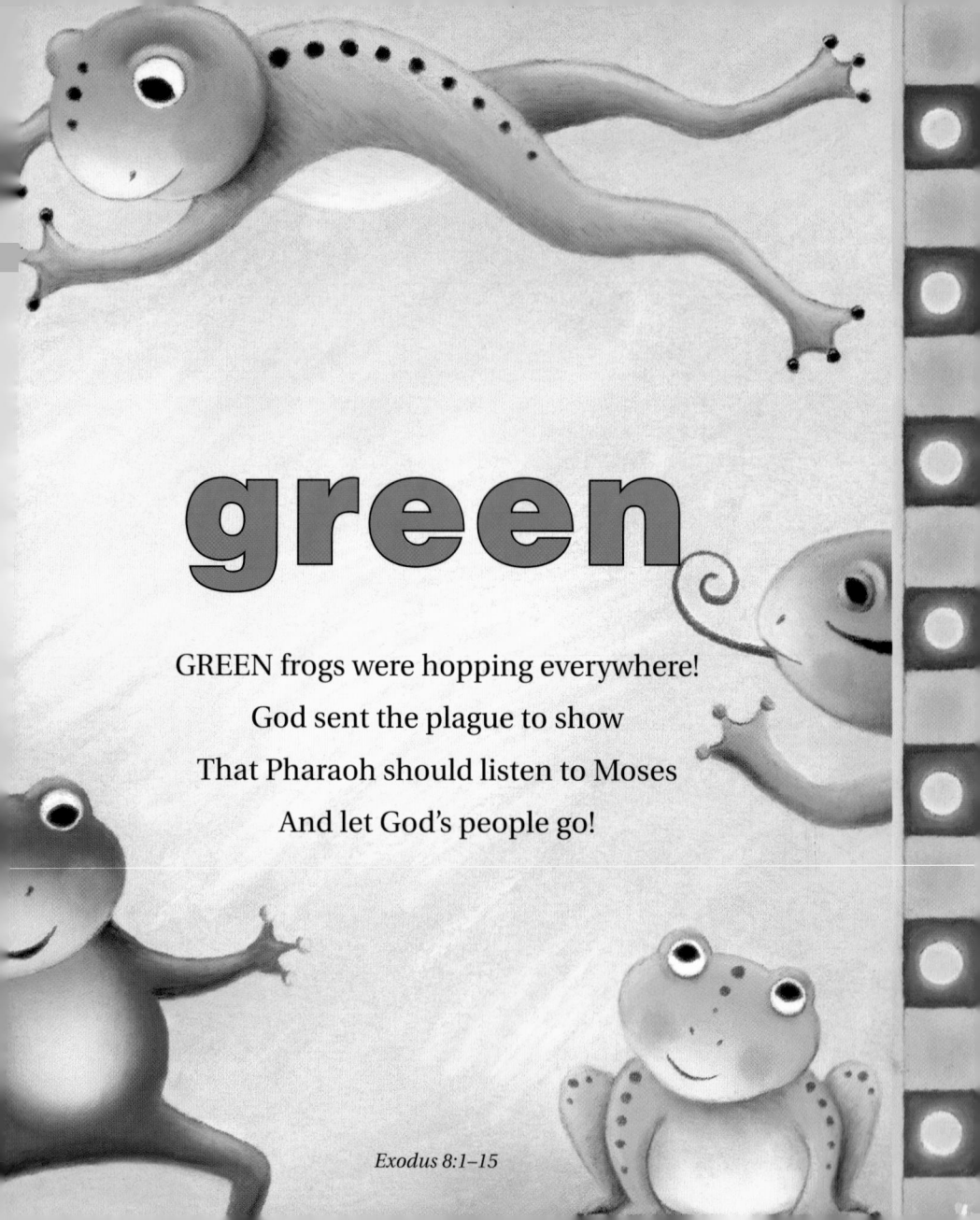

green

GREEN frogs were hopping everywhere!

God sent the plague to show

That Pharaoh should listen to Moses

And let God's people go!

Exodus 8:1–15

red

See the shiny RED apple?
Adam and Eve took a bite.
They disobeyed the Lord's command
And knew it wasn't right.

Genesis 3:1–7

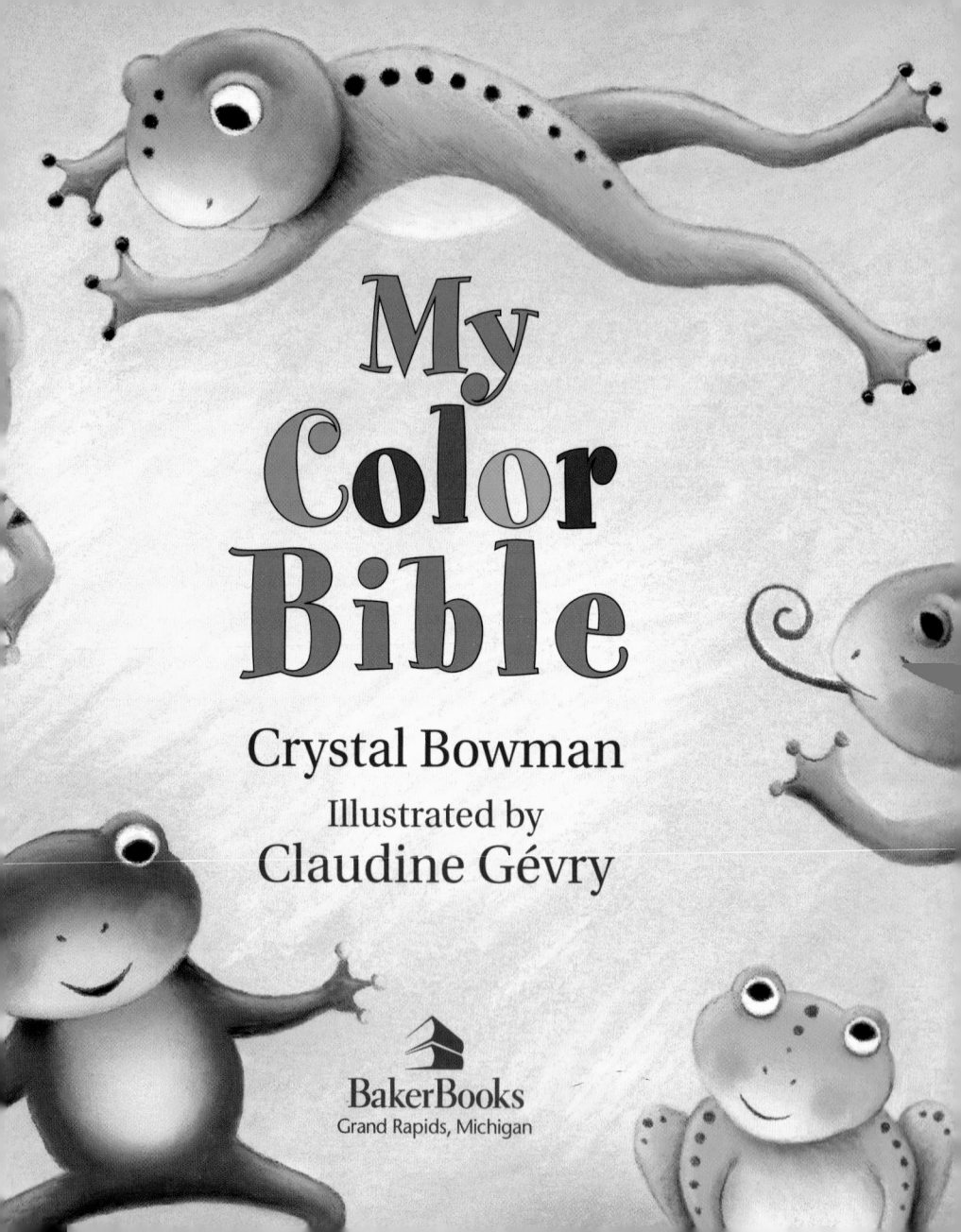

My Color Bible

Crystal Bowman

Illustrated by
Claudine Gévry

BakerBooks

Grand Rapids, Michigan